Kip and Zara's Money Adventure

For Diane and Evan.

B.R.

*Love to G for your never-ending inspiration
and thanks to Bill for this wonderful adventure!*

L.H.

Second printing, January 2007
Copyright ©2006 by PowerPlay Strategies Inc.

Published in Canada by
PowerPlay Strategies Inc.
PO Box 45034, Ocean Park RPO
Surrey, British Columbia
V4A 9L1

PowerPlay Strategies Inc. would like to thank Peter Herzog, Sandra Pike,
Brad Schmidt and Jorge Rocha for their support with this project.

The book was designed in Adobe PageMaker.
The illustrations were scanned and rendered in Adobe Photoshop.
Text is set in Garamond.

Cover edited by Heidi McCurdy
Printed and bound in Canada by Friesens

Library and Archives Canada Cataloguing in Publication
Roche, Bill, 1964-
Kip and Zara's money adventure / written by Bill Roche; illustrated and designed by Lyn Hart.
ISBN 0-9780028-0-6
I. Hart, Lyn, 1957-   II. Title.
PS8635.O284K56 2006   jC813'.6   C2006-900126-X

Kip and Zara's Money Adventure

Written by
Bill Roche

Illustrated by
Lyn Hart

PowerPLAY
strategies inc.

Zara was meeting Kip at the space station. It was a big day. The two young aliens were going dome camping in the jungle on Planet Zorlu. It was the first time they were allowed to go on a trip all by themselves.

"What's wrong, Kip?" said Zara. "You look really sad."

"I can't go," said Kip. "I spent all my money at the laser arcade."

Zara looked annoyed. "What do you mean?" she said. "That money was for your camping supplies."

"I'm really sorry," said Kip. "I thought my mom would pay for my trip, but she said I have to live with my spending decisions."

"Hey, Kip," said Zara, "you still have time to earn money to pay for your supplies."

"Great idea," said Kip. "I really want to go camping."

"Well, I'll meet you back here later," said Zara. "I'm going to play."

6

"But Zara," cried Kip, "how can I earn money?"

"Don't worry. You'll find a way," said Zara as she headed off for the clubhouse.

"Oh," sighed Kip, "I wish I could play, too. If only I hadn't wasted my money."

Kip walked toward the jetport where the rockets took off for the far parts of the universe. He wondered how he could earn money.

"Hey, Kip!" a voice called. It was his friend Galactupus with a pile of supply packs for a trip.

"Will you please help me carry these?" asked Galactupus. "I'm afraid I will miss my rocket."

Kip was a kind little alien. He picked up three packs and headed toward the rocket.

"Thank you!" said Galactupus. "I'll pay you three spondoolees for helping me."

Wow! Kip thought. *Maybe I could earn money by carrying luggage. I have lots of friends here who might need help.*

"Zara! Zara!" Kip shouted as he burst into the clubhouse. "I spent all morning earning money at the jetport!"

He poured a pile of spondoolees onto the table. Zara counted them.

"Now you have enough money for your trip," she smiled.

"Whoopee!" Kip was so excited, he ran across the ceiling twice.

"What are these?" said Kip pointing to the three pouches on Zara's belt. Each pouch had a different label.

"Money is for spending, giving and growing," said Zara, "so I keep my money in three pouches."

"My money is all for spending," said Kip. "I'll just keep mine in my pocket."

"Let's go shopping," said Kip.
They ran over to Space Market.

"Here is a list of supplies you'll need," said Zara, as she passed Kip a micro-note.

Zara went into the store. Kip stopped outside to see his favourite treats in the window.

Hmm . . . maybe I'll just buy Moon Crunch, Kip thought.

He quickly changed the list and then joined Zara inside.

15

Kip and Zara arrived back at the space station just in time to board the space roamer.

"This is exciting!" Zara shouted as they zoomed out of the station. "Planet Zorlu's jungle has the biggest trees in the entire galaxy . . . and the most unusual creatures!"

"I feel sick," muttered Kip. He had already eaten a whole package of Moon Crunch.

"Hey, Kip, I saw a new griggle detector at Space Market," said Zara. "I really wanted to buy it, but I didn't have enough money left in my spending pouch."

"But Zara," said Kip, "you still have money in your other two pouches."

"That money is for giving and growing," said Zara. "I won't spend that."

It didn't take long to reach
the jungle and find a good dome site.
"Don't forget to spray your dome
with anti-griggle spray,"
said Zara.

Kip felt a little embarrassed. "I . . . I . . . I didn't buy any spray," he said. "I only bought Moon Crunch."

Zara shook her head. "Let's hope there aren't any griggles. I only have enough spray for my dome."

Night was beginning to fall.
Kip went to find some water
to drink with dinner.

On his way back, he heard
a strange hissing noise. He
hoped it wasn't a griggle. Then
his flashlight began to flicker.
"Oh, no," he whispered
and dived into the bushes.

"Kip?" It was Zara. "What's taking you so long?"

Kip jumped up.

"Hey, why didn't you use your flashlight?" asked Zara.

"Oh, I didn't need it," said Kip, trying to sound brave. "I'm not afraid of the dark."

Kip was looking forward
to a good meal.

"I already ate," said Zara,
as they got back to their site.
"What did you bring for dinner?"

Kip looked in his backpack.
He couldn't eat any more Moon
Crunch, no matter what.

"I'm not hungry," he said.

Kip crawled into his dome. He was sticky and dirty and was beginning to wish he'd bought some soap after all. He was just about to fall asleep when he heard the tiny footsteps of griggles . . .

The next day Kip woke up covered in purple spots.

"The griggles found you very tasty," laughed Zara.

"Those spots won't last long, but they will be really itchy today," said the blarg who was standing with Zara. Blargs are the unusual creatures who live in Planet Zorlu's jungle.

"This is Varg, my money coach," said Zara. "She helps me find the best places for my money to grow."

"Money grows?" said Kip. "I don't understand."

"We'll show you how it works," said Varg.

They started walking toward Blarg Village.

The three aliens stopped at the Star Fruit Company.

"On Zara's last visit, she invested some of her growing money in this business," said Varg.

"That means I own a share of the Star Fruit Company," explained Zara. "When they sell all this fruit, my share will be worth more spondoolees."

"If you continue to find good places for your money to grow," said Varg, "you'll have even more spondoolees in the future."

"I'm going to have a million spondoolees when I grow up," said Zara.

"Me, too," said Kip.

"Not if you keep spending all your money on Moon Crunch," said Zara.

Kip and Zara met their friend Carmichael nearby. He was trying to take medicine to the jungle to help sick animals.

"What's wrong with your space roamer?" asked Kip.

"I need a new jet-blaster," he said, "but I don't have enough money to buy one."

Kip wanted to help, but he had no spondoolees.

Zara took the spondoolees from
her giving pouch and gave them
to Carmichael. "I am donating this money
to help the animals," she said.

"Oh, thank you!" called Carmichael
as he hurried off to buy the part.

Thanks to Zara, the space roamer was quickly fixed and ready to take the medicine to the animal shelter.

Zara was happy to help. At that moment,
Kip wished he had a giving pouch, too.

After a fun day of exploring, Kip and Zara took the space roamer back to the space station.

"I have an idea," said Kip. He took three empty Moon Crunch boxes from his backpack and wrote the words spend, give and grow on them.

"Now you have your own money system," said Zara.

"That's right," said Kip. "And now I'm ready for our next money adventure."

Welcome to
Kip and Zara's Money Activities!

Have fun with your own money adventures. Kip and Zara will show you how with the activities in this section. There are even tips for parents so they can help you get started.

ACTIVITY
Making a Money System

Design your own money system at home. You can use three pots, jars, boxes or envelopes. Be creative. Decorate your pots and have fun!

When Kip told his parents about his spending, giving and growing boxes, they were very impressed. They agreed to give him three spondoolees every week— one for each box. This money is called an allowance.

ACTIVITY

Starting an Allowance

Talk to your parents about your money system. Ask them for an allowance and decide how much money will go into each of your three pots.

Parent Tips

The "three-pot" system helps children build healthy, long-term money management habits. Give your child a regular allowance and follow Kip and Zara's money system. Remember, to learn about money, a child needs to be using it.

ACTIVITY

Earning Money

Some aliens like to earn extra money. Think of ways that you could earn money on your planet. When you do earn money, remember to put some into each pot.

Kip and his parents signed an allowance contract, so they would remember how much money goes into each pot.

ACTIVITY

Signing a Contract

Make your system official. Complete and sign the allowance contract on the next page.

Allowance Contract

_____
your name

will receive _____
allowance amount

for an allowance every _____.
allowance day

_____
your name

agrees to put the following amounts
into each pot.

_____ _____ _____
Spending   Giving   Growing

Signed by:

_____
your name

_____
your parent's name

_____
date

© 2006 PowerPlay Strategies Inc.

39

One day, Kip and Zara went shopping as soon as they received their allowances. Kip used the money in his spending box to buy packages of Moon Crunch. Zara decided to save some of her spending money until she had enough to buy a griggle detector.

ACTIVITY

Making a Spending Plan

Make a list of things you would like to buy. Decide what you want most. Can you buy it now or will you have to save up your spending money?

Parent Tips

Help your child set and achieve spending goals. Encourage him or her to make spending decisions. Treat mistakes as learning opportunities.

Talk to your child about money. Important topics include:

- Good value—sometimes it's better to spend more on a product that will last longer.
- Demands on money such as rent, clothing, food and electricity.
- The importance of saving.

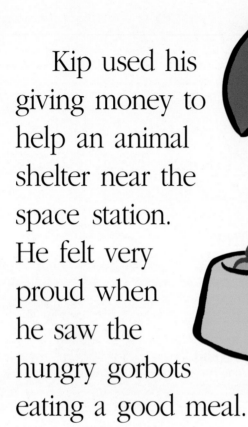

Kip used his giving money to help an animal shelter near the space station. He felt very proud when he saw the hungry gorbots eating a good meal.

ACTIVITY

Helping Others

Make a list of ways you can use the money in your giving pot to help others. Always remember to get your parents' permission before talking with strangers.

Zara bought flowers with her giving money. She and her dad took the flowers to a blarg who had just moved to their planet.

At first Zara felt a little shy, but she quickly relaxed and enjoyed meeting her new neighbour.

Parent Tips

Help your child develop a passion for giving. Plan a project and help him or her experience the joy of giving. Look for opportunities to help your child build confidence and people skills along the way.

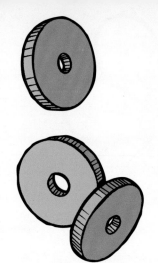

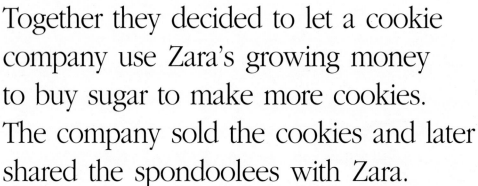

Zara met with
Varg to talk about
her growing money.
Together they decided to let a cookie
company use Zara's growing money
to buy sugar to make more cookies.
The company sold the cookies and later
shared the spondoolees with Zara.

She then had even more
spondoolees in her
growing pot.

Making Money Grow

Start saving your growing money. A money coach can help you find the best places for your money to grow.

On Planet Earth, money coaches are called financial advisors.

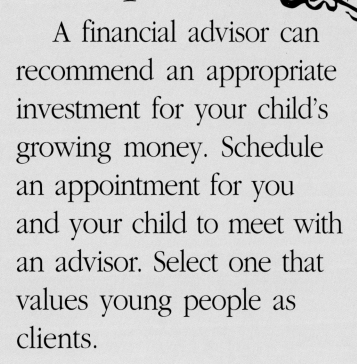

Parent Tips

A financial advisor can recommend an appropriate investment for your child's growing money. Schedule an appointment for you and your child to meet with an advisor. Select one that values young people as clients.

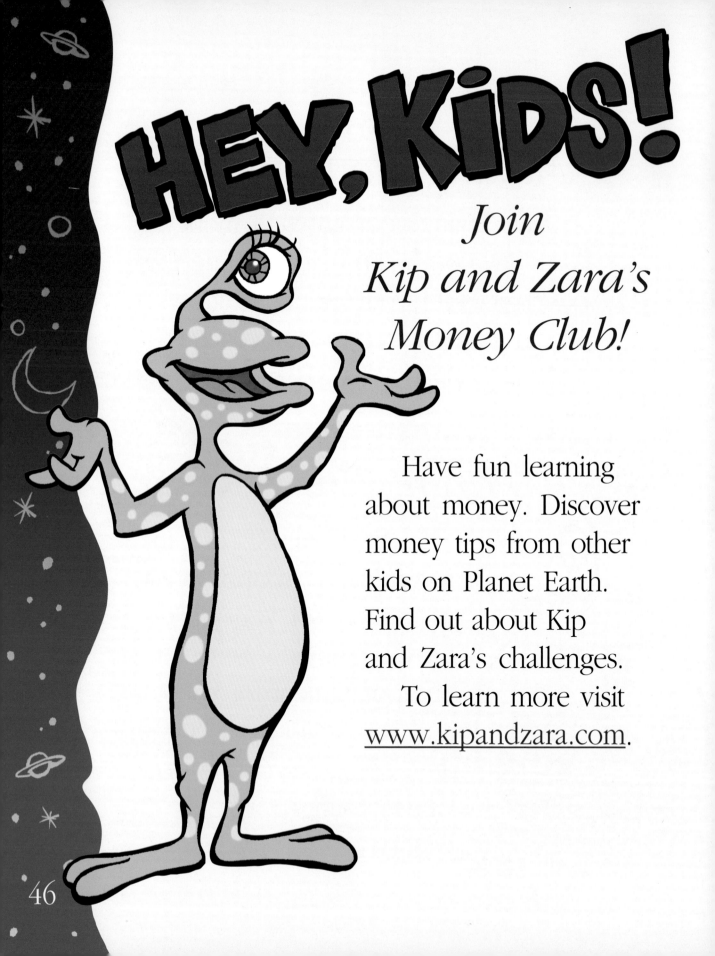

HEY, KIDS!

Join Kip and Zara's Money Club!

Have fun learning about money. Discover money tips from other kids on Planet Earth. Find out about Kip and Zara's challenges. To learn more visit www.kipandzara.com.

Kip and Zara want to hear from you!

- What tips do you have for spending money?
- How do you make your money grow?
- Do you know ways for kids to earn money?
- What are some fun giving projects?

Contact Kip and Zara . . .

By mail:
Kip and Zara
c/o PowerPlay Strategies Inc.
PO Box 45034, Ocean Park RPO
Surrey, BC, Canada   V4A 9L1

By e-mail:
moneyclub@kipandzara.com

47

A Message from Author Bill Roche

Dear Parents:

Kip and Zara's Money Adventure is one of many resources offered by PowerPlay Strategies Inc.

This entertaining storybook is a fun way to introduce important money concepts to children. The greatest and longest-lasting value will come from applying the concepts at home. Use the creative activity section to help your child discover how money works.

We recommend you visit www.powerplay4success.com. This family website offers tips for parents and a variety of resources for helping children and youth develop practical life skills and positive beliefs about money.

Congratulations on your progress! And thank you for joining us on this journey. See you in our future adventures.

Sincerely,

Bill Roche

Author and Founder of PowerPlay Strategies Inc.